What James Likes Best

amy schwartz

A Richard Jackson Book
Atheneum Books for Young Readers
New York London Toronto Sydney Singapore

The Twins

One fine day, James goes to visit the twins.

James and Mommy and Daddy ride on

an express bus. It is white with green stripes.

They get off at a red brick house.

There are two babies inside.

The babies are the same size.

They are twins. They can't walk yet

and they can't talk yet.

They have

two rocking horses,

two jack-in-the-boxes,

two toy clowns,

two train engines,

and two toy telephones.

The twins eat lunch in two white high chairs.

They say, "Mmmmmmm, mmmmm, mmmmm."

James sits on Mommy's lap and eats a cookie,

an ice cream, and a doughnut hole.

Then James and Mommy and Daddy say good-bye and ride the express bus home.

And what do you think James liked best?

Was it the two toy telephones?

Or the two toy clowns?

Or the express bus?

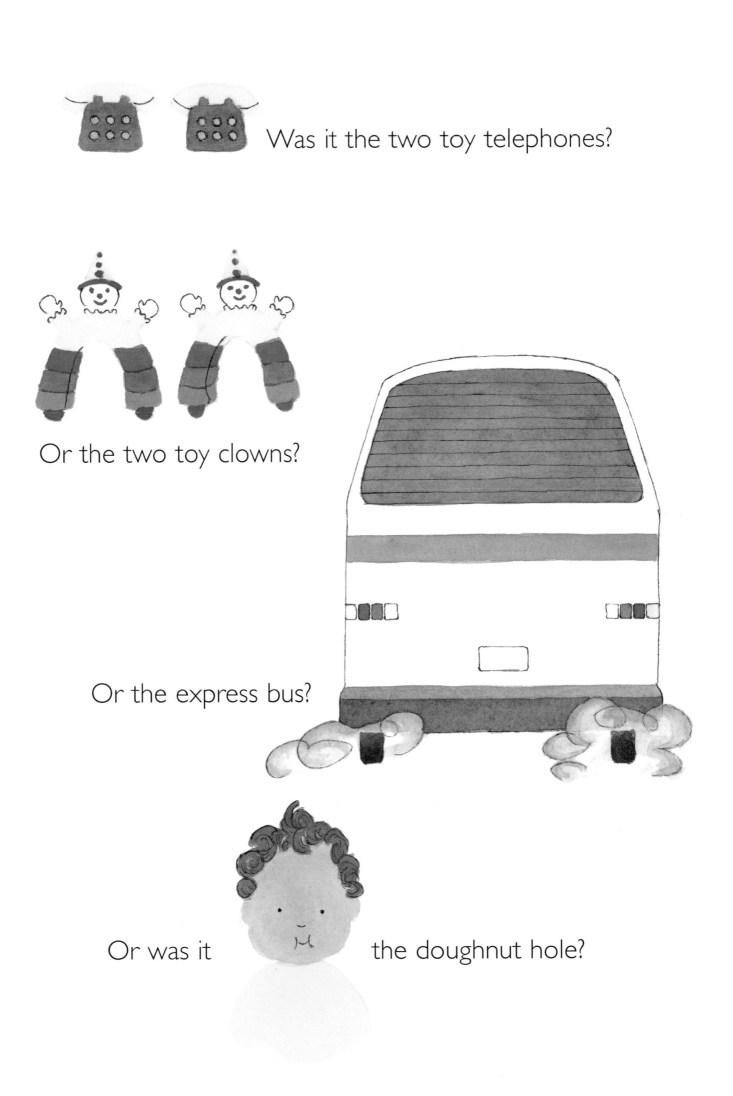

Or was it the doughnut hole?

Grandma's House

One rainy day, James and Mommy and Daddy
visit Grandma and Auntie.
They take a taxi to Grandma's house.

James finds the kitchen,

the bathroom, and the den.

Grandma gives him a purple car.

James plays cards with Auntie.

She has funny hair.

James eats a piece of
cheese with a little fork.

He tries on hats

and plays the king.

Everybody hugs and kisses.
Then James and Mommy and
Daddy take a taxi home.

And what do you think James liked best?

Was it the purple car?

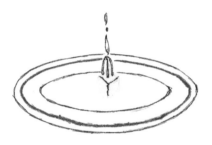 Or the the little fork?

Or the taxi?

Or was it Auntie's funny hair?

The County Fair

One Sunday James goes to the County Fair.

He gets up before the sun.

Mommy and Daddy and James go to a garage

and get into a yellow car.

Mommy turns on the windshield wipers.

On and off, on and off, on and off.

"Oops," Mommy says.

Then Mommy drives the car to the County Fair.

At the fair, they eat corn on the cob, cotton candy, and pretzels.

They visit goats, two sheep, and a pig.

James pets a green snake.

He doesn't ride on a pony.

But he does ride on a train with Daddy.

Around and around and around.

James waves to Mommy.

And what do you think James liked best?

Was it the corn on the cob?

Or the green snake?

Or the train?

Or was it the windshield wipers?

Angela

One morning, James and Mommy go on a playdate.

James puts on his sweatshirt and his coat with a hood.

They walk next door to Angela's house.

James takes off his sweatshirt

and his coat with a hood.

He eats a muffin.

Then James plays in Angela's toy kitchen.

It has toy pots, toy pans, and a toy stove.

"Look," Angela's mommy says.

A robin hops by outside.

James and Angela go upstairs.

Angela has toy fruit.

James and Angela throw fruit

down the stairs.

      Apples,

          bananas,

             and oranges.

"Time to go now," Mommy says.

James puts on his sweatshirt

and his coat with a hood.

"Good-bye Angela."

"Good-bye James."

And what do you think
James liked best?

Was it the robin?

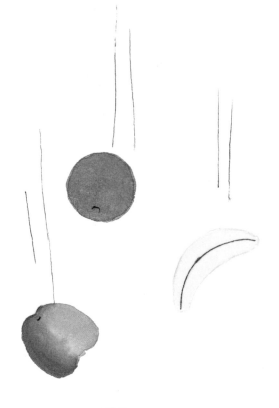

Or the toy fruit?

Or the muffin?

Or was it Angela?

For Jacob

Atheneum Books for Young Readers
An imprint of Simon & Schuster Children's Publishing Division
1230 Avenue of the Americas
New York, New York 10020

Book design by Kristin Smith
The text of this book is set in GillSans.
The illustrations are rendered in gouache and pen-and-ink.
Manufactured in China
First Edition
10 9 8 7 6 5 4 3 2 1
Library of Congress Cataloging-in-Publication Data
Schwartz, Amy.
What James likes best / Amy Schwartz.
p.   cm.
"A Richard Jackson book."
Summary: A little boy goes with his parents on an express bus
to visit twins, in a taxi to visit Grandma, and in a car to see the
county fair, then walks next door with his mother for a playdate.
ISBN 0-689-84059-4
[1. Transportation—Fiction. 2. Family—Fiction.] I. Title.
PZ7.S406 Wh 2003
[E]—dc21   2001022988